for Iwan,
Jem, Sam, Finn,
and Zac

tiger tales
an imprint of ME Media, LLC
5 River Road, Suite 128, Wilton, CT 06897
Published in the United States 2013
Originally published in Great Britain 2012
by Red Fox Books
an imprint of Random House Children's Books
Text and illustrations copyright © 2012 Kali Stileman
CIP data is available
LPP 0612
ISBN-13: 978-1-58925-127-4
ISBN-10: 1-58925-127-X
Printed in China
1 3 5 7 9 10 8 6 4 2

For more insight and activities,
visit us at www.tigertalesbooks.com

Snack Time for Confetti

by Kali Stileman

tiger tales

Confetti was

HUNGRY!!!

Really, really hungry!

"I'm hungry," said Confetti
to Jemima Giraffe.

"I love to eat luscious,
lip-smacking leaves,"
said the giraffe. "Try some."

"Yum!" said the giraffe.

"Yuck!" said Confetti.

"I'm hungry," said Confetti
to Zoey Zebra.

"I eat sweet green grass,"
said the zebra. "Try some."

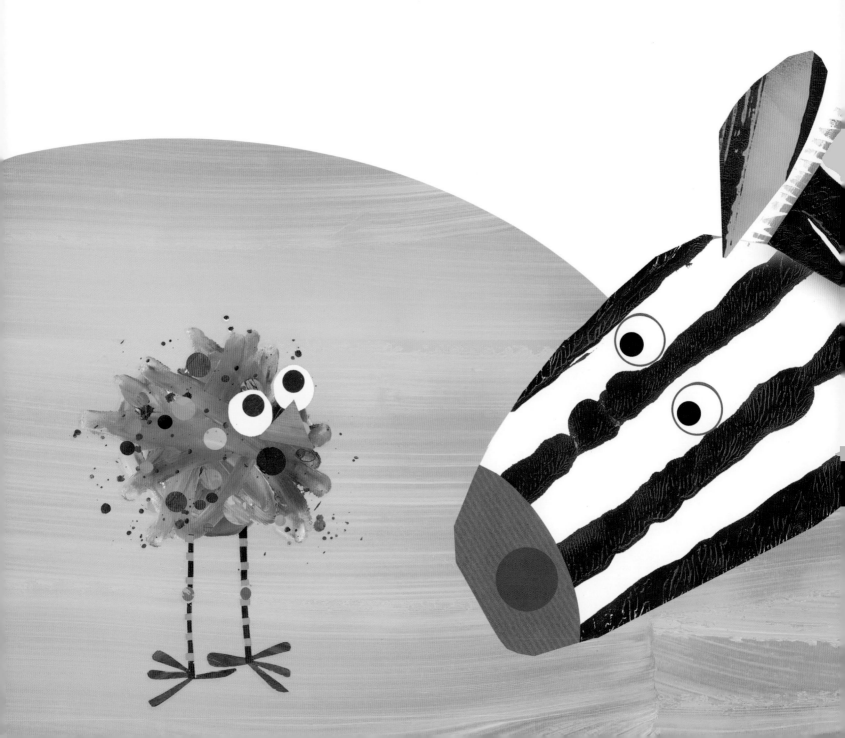

"Yum!" said the zebra.

"Yuck!" said Confetti.

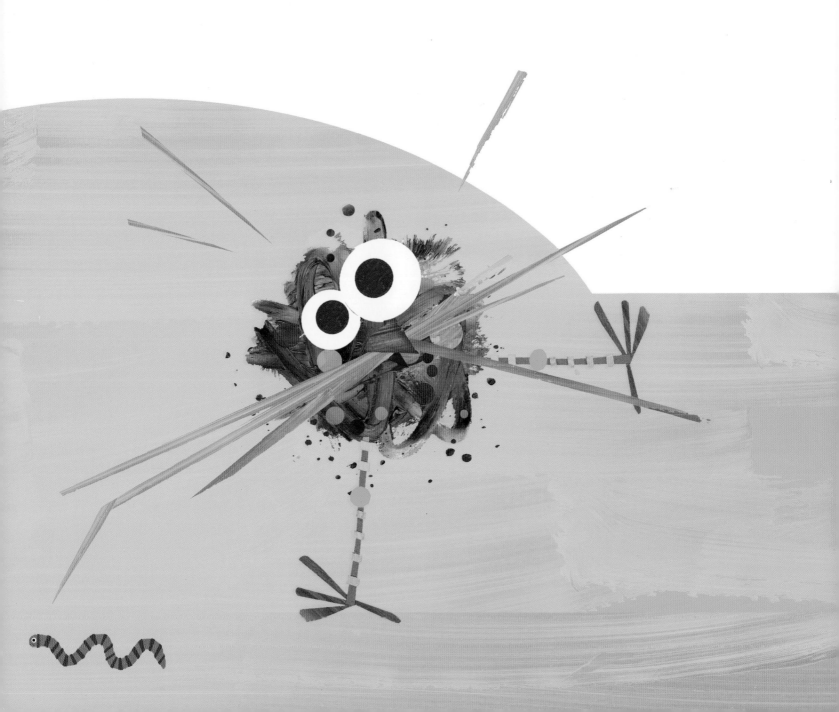

"I'm hungry," said Confetti
to Emma Elephant.

"I eat lots and lots of fabulous fruits and vegetables," said the elephant. "Try some."

"Yum!" said the elephant.

"Yuck!" said Confetti.

"I'm hungry," said Confetti to Christopher Crocodile.

"So am I!" said the crocodile.

"But maybe not that hungry," she whispered.

"I'm hungry," said Confetti to Madison Monkey.

"I eat nice delicious nuts," said the monkey. "Try some."

"Yum!" said the monkey.
"Yuck!" said Confetti.

Confetti's mom came home with . . .

a wiggly worm,

a **beautiful** beetle,

a *speedy* spider,

a creeping,
crawling caterpillar,

and a **skinny** stick insect.

"Yum!"
said Confetti.

"Yuck!"
said all the other animals.